Nicely

For the other Angela (Lucey) – with thanks for everything ~ A M

For cupcake lovers everywhere ~ D R

STRIPES PUBLISHING
An imprint of Little Tiger Press
1 The Coda Centre, 189 Munster Road,
London SW6 6AW

A paperback original
First published in Great Britain in 2016

ISBN: 978-1-84715-600-6

A CIP catalogue record for this book is available from the British Library.

Printed and bound in the UK.

10 9 8 7 6 5 4 3 2 1

Angela Nicely

Cupcake Wars!

ALAN MACDONALD ILLUSTRATED BY DAVID ROBERTS

Stripes

Have you read the other
Angela Nicely books?

Contents

Cupcake
Wars!

Chapter 1

Angela's class sat cross-legged on the carpet. This morning Miss Darling had something important she wanted to talk about.

"Can anyone tell me what's happening on Saturday March 21st?" she asked. "Yes, Tiffany?"

Tiffany Charmers' hand was up.

"The Spring Fair!" she cried.

"Well done, Tiffany," said Miss Darling. "It's the Spring Fair and we need lots of exciting stalls. We've already got a lucky dip, face painting and a toy stall, but what else could we have?"

"A dinosaur stall," cried the twins.

"A Spiderman stall!" shouted Spike.

"They're both lovely ideas, but they might be difficult," said Miss Darling. "Try to think of things we can bring into school or make ourselves. Jewellery or badges, for instance."

Angela had come up with a brilliant idea, something that was a certain winner. She turned to Laura and whispered it. But Tiffany overheard and raised her hand.

"Yes, Tiffany?" said Miss Darling.

"A CAKE STALL!" cried Tiffany, smirking at Angela.

"That's a marvellous idea!" said Miss Darling. "I'm sure we can make some lovely cakes with the help of your parents."

Angela looked daggers at Tiffany. A cake stall was HER idea. Trust Tiffany to steal it! She must have been earwigging as usual. She couldn't stand anyone else winning praise, especially if it happened to be Angela. Tiffany always had to be top at everything.

"Well, keep thinking," said Miss Darling as the bell went. "And we'll need lots of helpers to run the stalls, so I'll be looking for vounteers."

Angela stomped outside to the playground. She was still hopping mad with Tiffany.

"It's so unfair!" she stormed. "The cake stall was my idea. Tiffany stole it!"

"We'll just have to think of something else," said Maisie.

Laura sighed. "Tiffany always gets her own way."

"Well, not this time," said Angela. "We should run our own cake stall."

"But we don't have any cakes," Maisie pointed out.

"So? We could make them," said Angela. "My mum makes amazing cakes – ginger, lemon, chocolate fudge..."

"Cupcakes!" cried Laura suddenly.

They both looked at her.

"Everyone likes cupcakes! And you could make loads of them," she explained.

Angela's eyes shone. It wasn't such a bad idea. They could make all different cupcakes – chocolatey, lemony, strawberry, banana-ey, even heart-shaped ones.

Chapter 2

Later on, Miss Darling drew up a list of stalls and took the names of the children who wanted to help. Some of the class had stalls in mind, while others were happy to help with anything.

"What about you, Angela?" asked Miss Darling.

"I'm running a cake stall with Maisie

and Laura," said Angela firmly.

Tiffany stared. "YOU CAN'T!" she squawked. "I'm doing a cake stall. It was my idea!"

"I thought of it first," said Angela.

"You did NOT!" cried Tiffany.

"I did, you stole my idea!" said Angela.

Tiffany pulled a face. "LIAR, LIAR, PANTS ON FIRE!" she sang.

"Girls, girls!" sighed Miss Darling, holding up her hands. "It really doesn't matter who thought of it first. If you both want to run a cake stall, why don't you do it together?"

Tiffany stuck her nose in the air. No way was she working with that big-mouth Angela. Angela folded her arms. No way was she working with that snooty show-off Tiffany.

"Very well," groaned Miss Darling, giving up. "We'll have *two* cake stalls at the fair. I'm sure they'll both be a great success."

Tiffany smiled to herself. She knew whose cake stall would be the best.

Angela narrowed her eyes. *You wait,* she thought. *OUR cake stall's going to be the star of the fair.*

When Angela got home she found her mum in the kitchen on her laptop.

"Mum," she said. "You know cupcakes – are they easy to make?"

Mrs Nicely looked up. "Cupcakes? They're not difficult. Why?"

"Because I'm probably going to need a hundred," replied Angela.

"A HUNDRED?" cried Mrs Nicely. "What on earth for?"

"The Spring Fair," explained Angela. "Me, Laura and Maisie are running a cake stall – and it's got to be better than Tiffany's."

Mrs Nicely rolled her eyes. She might have known that Tiffany Charmers would be involved. Hardly a week went by without Mrs Charmers boasting about her daughter's latest brilliant achievement. Well, this time Tiffany wouldn't have it her own way.

"And who'll be making all these cupcakes?" Mrs Nicely asked.

"We will – me and my friends," answered Angela. "But we might need a teeny bit of help."

She threw her arms round her mum.

"Go on then," laughed Mrs Nicely. "As long as you help clear up and don't leave a mess."

"I promise!" cried Angela.

Chapter 3

The following week, Angela's friends came round for a baking session.

"Right," said Mrs Nicely. "I'll help you bake the cakes and you can decorate them yourselves."

She showed them how to measure out the flour, butter and sugar, tipping the ingredients into a mixing bowl.

Next Maisie and Laura cracked the eggs. Most of them went in the bowl. Then came the part Angela liked best – mixing with the electric whisk.

"Be careful," warned her mum. "Keep it on a low speed and don't spill any."

"I won't," Angela promised. This was as easy as one, two, three! She turned on the whisk, but somehow the dial was on "high speed". The whisk sprang into life…

DRRRRRRR!

"Not so fast!" cried Mrs Nicely, as Angela plunged the whisk into the mix.

Suddenly thick goo was flying everywhere, splatting the work top and the walls.

"TURN IT OFF! TURN IT OFF!" screamed Mrs Nicely.

Angela switched off the whisk and looked up. Laura and Maisie were dripping with yellow goo. Angela's mum had a big blob of cake mix on her nose. She folded her arms.

"Ooops!" said Angela.

Mrs Nicely decided it would be safer to finish the mixing herself. Maisie and Laura spooned the mixture into paper cases, then the cupcakes went in the oven to bake. When they were ready, Mrs Nicely took them out and left them to cool down.

"Right, I'm going to get changed," she said. "You can start on the icing. I've left everything out on the table."

Angela inspected the cupcakes. Some seemed to have sunk in the middle or drooped to one side.

"They don't look very exciting," she grumbled.

"We haven't decorated them yet," Laura reminded her.

"I think they'll look great," said Maisie. "I'm using pink icing."

"I'm using yellow," said Laura.

But Angela still wasn't happy. She wanted cakes that would make Tiffany squirm with envy. But how to make them super-special? She eyed the bottles of food colouring and smiled.

"RAINBOW CUPCAKES!" she cried.

"Rainbow?" said Laura.

"Yes, they'll look fantastic!" said Angela.

They began decorating their cakes. Angela blobbed on some red icing, then added a line of yellow, orange and purple. Arghhh! All the colours were running together in a big blobby mess! Maybe it would be less fiddly to mix up the rainbow icing in a bowl?

Twenty minutes later, the cupcakes were finished. Maisie's cupcakes were pretty pink, Laura's were pale yellow while Angela's were ... hard to describe.

"EWW! They look disgusting!" cried Maisie.

"What have you done, Angela?" moaned Laura.

"It's not my fault!" wailed Angela. "They're meant to be rainbow cupcakes!"

It turned out that if you mixed lots of colours together in a bowl the result was a muddy messy brown.

"What are we going to do?" sighed Maisie. "We've used up all the icing."

"At least *ours* look nice," said Laura. "And I'm sure Angela's taste better than they look."

Angela stared miserably at her blobby cupcakes. She could just imagine what Tiffany would say: "Oh, ANG-ER-LA, you are hopeless! What do you call those? Mud pies?"

On the day of the fair, Angela and her friends arrived early to set up. Miss Darling showed them to one of the tables.

"We certainly won't be short of cakes!" she laughed. "You should see how many Tiffany's made."

Angela set down her tins and marched over to inspect her rival's work. Tiffany and Alice had arranged their cakes in four neat rows – pink, lavender, lemon and strawberry. Angela stared in disbelief.

"CUPCAKES?" she howled.

"Aren't they just perfect?" smiled Tiffany.

"But *we're* selling cupcakes!" cried Angela.

"No you're not," said Tiffany. "Cupcakes were my idea."

"They were not! You copied us again!" howled Angela.

Miss Darling heard the argument and hurried over.

"How are we getting on, girls?" she asked.

Tiffany folded her arms. "Miss, tell Angela she can't sell cupcakes," she said.

"And tell Tiffany we thought of it first," replied Angela.

Miss Darling was losing patience. "I'm sure it'll be fine," she said. "Everyone likes cupcakes and they can choose whichever they want."

"Obviously they'll all want mine!" said Tiffany smugly.

"We'll see about that," said Angela.

"Anyway, people will be here soon," said Miss Darling. "Let's just get ready, shall we?"

Angela stomped back to her friends. Tiffany was unbelievable! She must have heard their idea and copied them on purpose. It was obvious she hadn't baked or decorated the cakes herself, either. They were so neat and perfect they could only be Mrs Charmers' work.

Chapter 4

Slowly the school hall filled up with visitors. Maisie had set out their cakes in three rows – candy pink, buttercup yellow and sludgy brown. People stopped to look but moved on quickly when they saw Angela's cakes. Lots of them went to Tiffany's stall instead. After half an hour, Angela had sold

one cake to her dad, and Maisie and Laura had sold just three between them. Meanwhile, Tiffany's stall had an enormous queue that never went down.

"It's not fair!" grumbled Maisie. "Tiffany's stealing all our customers!"

Tiffany looked over and waved a five-pound note. *Right, you asked for it, this is war!* thought Angela. She picked up their price tag and crossed out "30".

"What are you doing?" asked Laura.

"Beating Tiffany," said Angela. "Just watch."

She climbed on to a chair and raised her voice above the noise.

"Special offer! Buy your cupcakes here: ONLY 20p!"

A girl stopped at their stall.

"Twenty?" she said. "Tiffany's charging thirty."

"I know – ours taste better, too," said Angela. "How many do you want?"

The girl bought two of Maisie's pink cupcakes. Soon their stall was doing a brisk trade. Tiffany ground her teeth. But two could play at that game. She sent Alice to find her a chair to stand on.

"Get your name on a cupcake!" she cried. "Only at Tiffany's cake stall!"

Angela frowned. "What's she doing now?"

"Writing people's names in icing," replied Laura.

"Huh, big deal! Who wants their name on a cupcake?" scoffed Angela.

"Looks like lots of people do," replied Maisie.

Tiffany's named cupcakes proved a winning idea. Meanwhile Angela's stall had sold all their pink and yellow cupcakes, but that still left dozens of muddy brown cakes that no one wanted.

Laura sat down. "Face it," she sighed. "Tiffany's won."

"Laura's right," agreed Maisie. "No one's going to buy these. They look like blobby monsters!"

Angela stared at the rows of mud-coloured cakes. Actually they did look a bit like monsters. Her eyes lit up –

maybe that was the answer!

"Wait here, I'll be back in a minute!" she said.

Laura and Maisie looked at each other. What was Angela up to now?

Soon she was back with a bag of Gummy Shapes from the sweet stall. Angela pushed a pair of pink teeth into one of the brown cupcakes. She added a gummy nose and two goggly eyes, then held it up.

"Wow! That looks scary!" said Laura.

"We're not beaten yet," said Angela, climbing back on to her chair.

"Monster cupcakes! Make a monster cake!" she yelled, holding up the one she'd made. People turned their heads and laughed. The cupcake looked exactly like a goggle-eyed monster.

Angela's neighbour, Bertie, hurried over with his friends, Darren and Eugene.

"I'll have one!" he said. "Can we make our own?"

"Help yourself," said Angela.

"Great," said Darren. "My monster's having three eyes."

"Mine's got fangs!" said Eugene.

The monster faces attracted crowds of eager children.

"That's the last one," said Laura, serving a little girl.

30p

Maisie grinned at Angela. "Your mud pies were a big hit after all!" she said.

When the fair drew to an end, they counted their money.

"Almost twenty pounds!" said Laura.

Looking up, they saw Tiffany marching towards them. She had red cheeks and a furious scowl.

"Oh, hello Tiffany," smiled Angela. "I'm afraid you're a bit too late."

"Yes, did you want a monster face?" asked Laura.

Angela giggled. "It's okay," she said. "I think Tiffany's got her own!"

Pony Party!
1

Chapter 1

It was Monday morning and Angela's class had gathered together for News Time.

"Now," said Miss Darling when they were quiet, "who has some news they'd like to share?"

"Ooh, Miss, Miss!" A dozen hands shot into the air. Angela waved her arm madly. In front of her, Tiffany Charmers was sitting up nicely and not calling out.

"Yes, Tiffany, what's your news?" said Miss Darling.

Angela slumped forward. *Tiffany, always Tiffany!*

"It's my birthday!" said Tiffany proudly.

"Oh, happy birthday!" said Miss Darling. "Is it today?"

Tiffany shook her head. "No, it's on Saturday. And guess what, I'm having a pony party at the stables."

Angela rolled her eyes. Everyone else had a party at their house or maybe at the swimming pool, but that wasn't good enough for Tiffany. Angela bet that any minute she'd start talking about her pony.

"I'll be riding my pony – her name's Princess," boasted Tiffany.

"Yes, I think you may have mentioned her before," smiled Miss Darling. "Well, I hope you have a lovely party, Tiffany."

"I will," said Tiffany. "All my friends are coming. I've got lots of friends."

Angela caught Maisie's eye and raised her eyebrows. There was no way she'd be getting an invitation. Tiffany and Angela were not best friends – Angela often said they were best enemies.

At break time, Angela sat on a bench with Maisie and Laura.

"I see Tiffany's handing out her invitations," sniffed Maisie. "Sophie got one."

Angela pulled a face. "I don't want one of her smelly invitations," she said.

"Nor me," agreed Laura.

"Me neither," said Maisie. "I wouldn't go to her party if you paid me a million, billion pounds."

"I wouldn't go if Tiffany got down on her knees and begged me," vowed Angela. "Who wants to go to a dopey pony party anyway?"

To tell the truth, Angela had never been to a pony party so she wasn't exactly sure what it involved. Did the ponies eat birthday cake, play games and wear party hats? In any case, Angela told herself, she didn't care that she wasn't invited – not one tiny little bit. Although come to think of it, it would be fun to ride a pony.

Just then the birthday girl appeared, twirling towards them on tippy-toes.

"Hello Ang-er-la!" cooed Tiffany. "What are you doing this Saturday?"

Angela shrugged. "Seeing Laura and Maisie, I expect," she said.

"Oh, that's a pity," said Tiffany, "because I wanted to give you this."

She handed over a sparkly card decorated with stars and balloons.

Angela opened it and almost fell off the bench in shock.

Dear Angela,
Please come to my Pony Party on Saturday 4th June at 2pm.
Dress for riding. See ya there!
Tiffany

Angela read the invitation again. Was this a joke?

"You're inviting ME?" she gasped.

"Well, duh! That's your name on the invitation," said Tiffany. "But wait, you've never been riding, have you?"

"No, but I could learn," said Angela.

"'Of course you could, silly, it's easy!" laughed Tiffany. "So you'll come?"

"Um ... yes," mumbled Angela.

"Super dooper!" cried Tiffany. "I'll see you on Saturday then. I can't wait!"

She gave a little laugh and skipped off across the playground.

Maisie and Laura stared at Angela with their mouths hanging open.

"WHAT?" said Angela. "Well, I could hardly say 'No', could I?"

Chapter 2

Over supper that evening, Angela told her parents about the invitation.

"From Tiffany?" said Mrs Nicely. "A pony party?"

"Yes," said Angela. "It's a party with ponies."

"I know what it is," said Mrs Nicely. "But why are you going? I thought you didn't like Tiffany."

"I don't," said Angela. "But I do like ponies."

"Well, I'm sure it'll be great fun," said Mr Nicely, who said that about everything.

Mrs Nicely wasn't convinced. "It doesn't say what you'll be doing," she said.

"Riding ponies," replied Angela. "Tiffany's got her own."

"That's all very well," said Mrs Nicely. "But aren't you forgetting that you've never ridden a horse in your life?"

Angela sighed. "Mu-um! Anyone can ride, it's easy!" she said. "If Tiffany can do it then I'm sure I can."

"Of course you can," said her dad. "Anyway, I'm sure there'll be people at the stables to help you."

Angela couldn't imagine she would need much help. After all, sitting on a horse couldn't be that different from sitting on a chair. And besides, she'd ridden a donkey at the seaside, so a pony wouldn't be any trouble. She'd probably turn out to be a natural. *After all,* she thought, *I'm quite good at most things.*

Her mum read the invitation again.

"Riding clothes!" she sighed. "What does that mean? Riding hats and jodhpurs, I suppose?"

"I've got joggers," said Angela.

"Jodhpurs," said her mum. "They're riding trousers."

"Can we buy some?" asked Angela.

"Certainly not," said her mum. "I'm not buying you expensive jodhpurs, just for Tiffany's party. You'll have to wear what you've got – jeans and boots."

"And I'm sure they'll have riding hats at the stables," said Dad.

Angela nodded. As long as she could go, she didn't mind if she had to dress as a Christmas tree. The truth was she'd always wanted to go riding, but her mum said that lessons were too expensive. She'd never dreamed that Tiffany of all people would give her the chance.

Angela frowned. *I wonder why she did invite me?* she thought. It wasn't like Tiffany to be so nice. Maisie said Tiffany was up to something, but that was only because she was jealous she hadn't been invited herself.

Chapter 3

On the day of the party, Angela's dad dropped her off at the riding stables. Angela could hardly contain her excitement. She couldn't wait to see which pony she would be riding.

Tiffany and the other girls were already in the yard with Mrs Charmers. Angela recognized Sophie, Alice and

Suki from her class. Her face fell when she saw that they were all wearing black hats, short jackets and smart cream jodhpurs. Angela was the only one dressed in old jeans and dirty wellies.

Tiffany shook her curly hair. "Oh Ang-er-la!" she sighed. "Didn't you read the invitation? It said come in riding clothes."

"But these are my riding clothes," said Angela.

"Jeans and wellies?" laughed Alice.

"And where's your riding hat?" asked Suki. "You can't ride without one."

"She can't help it," said Tiffany. "She doesn't even go riding, do you Ang-er-la?"

Angela hung her head. Why hadn't anyone warned her that wearing riding clothes mattered so much? Now she was the odd one out. And to make matters worse, it was obvious she was the only beginner. Angela wondered if that was why Tiffany had invited her in the first place – so they'd all have someone to laugh at.

"Never mind! You'll have to do," sighed Tiffany. "Come on, we'll find you a riding hat."

The girls trooped off to the stables. Angela had to borrow a hat. It was far too big and kept slipping down over her eyes.

Then it was time to saddle the horses. Mrs Charmers helped Tiffany with her little white pony.

"Daddy bought me Princess," Tiffany boasted. "She cost thousands but I just had to have her."

The other girls were all riding their favourite ponies. They had names like Blossom, Poppy and Bilbo. Angela stood helplessly watching them do complicated things with buckles and stirrups.

Tiffany put one foot in her stirrup and climbed on to Princess's back.

"Wait a minute, what about Angela?" said Mrs Charmers. "Which horse is she going to ride?"

The girls all looked at Angela. She certainly wasn't borrowing one of *their* horses.

"Who's left?" asked Alice.

"I know!" cried Tiffany. "Dobbin! He'd be perfect for you, Angela."

The other girls dissolved into giggles.

"Which one's Dobbin?" asked Angela, looking round.

One of the stable hands, Linda, went and brought him out. Angela stared. Dobbin wasn't a pony, he was a horse. A grey carthorse as big as a barn with ginormous hooves!

"But … but I can't ride *him*!" spluttered Angela.

"Of course you can," laughed Tiffany. "Anyone can ride Dobbin, even you, Ang-er-la!"

Angela thought that was easy for Tiffany to say. Princess was as dainty as a buttercup. Angela was going to need a stepladder to even get on Dobbin's back.

Chapter 4

Angela clung on to Dobbin's neck as Linda led the carthorse down to the paddock. She was scared to sit upright in case she fell off, but she didn't want to look down either – the ground was an awfully long way away. She'd probably be safer riding on an elephant!

"Hurry up, Angela!" called Tiffany.

"We're all waiting!"

At last they reached the paddock where everyone was standing in line. Tiffany smirked as she saw Angela's worried expression. There was a series of jumps set up around the paddock. Surely Tiffany had to be joking?

"Tiffany thought it would be fun to hold our own little gymkhana," said Mrs Charmers. "You can take it in turns to jump the course and whoever has the best round wins the prize." She held up a large red rosette.

"I've won hundreds of rosettes," Tiffany boasted. "My bedroom walls are practically covered in them."

Angela stared at the jumps. Most of them were bigger than her! And in any case, she couldn't imagine Dobbin managing to get off the ground.

"What about ME?" she said. "I've never jumped anything, not on a horse!"

Tiffany rolled her eyes. "Oh, don't make a fuss, Angela," she sighed. "You can just walk Dobbin round. We're not expecting you to win!"

"Not unless there's a prize for the slowest," said Alice, to a chorus of giggles.

Angela glared. That snooty sneak Tiffany had planned this from the start. She knew very well that Angela couldn't ride and was bound to trail in last. Now she'd have to listen to Tiffany telling everyone the story: "Poor Ang-er-la, she's just so hopeless!" she'd say.

Tiffany rode Princess into the paddock and trotted her round a couple of times to warm up. Leaning forward, she galloped hard at the first jump. Princess took off and jumped it perfectly.

"Go Tiffany!" cheered Mrs Charmers.

Tiffany completed the course without any fuss, only knocking down one pole among the jumps. She shook out her curly hair and waved her hat at them.

"Oh, well done, darling!" cried her mum. "You were so brave!"

Angela pulled a face. Knowing Tiffany, she'd probably practised the course a hundred times during the week. The competition was just another chance for her to show off and come top of the class as usual.

Alice, Suki and the others took their turns but none of them could match Tiffany's round. "Oh, bad luck!" she said, each time. "And you tried so hard!"

After seven rounds Tiffany was in the lead.

"Is that everyone?" she smirked. "Oh no! Does that mean I'm the winner?"

The other girls sat on the fence, sulking.

"What about Angela?" asked Alice.

"Oh yes, Ang-er-la!" cried Tiffany. "We mustn't forget you, must we?"

Angela gripped the reins. She would show that smarty-pants Tiffany. Linda led Dobbin into the ring as everyone leaned forward to watch. Dobbin snorted loudly. He'd seen the jumps and he didn't want to go near them. He dug in his hooves and stopped.

"Come on!" Angela hissed in his ear.

"Just walk him round, Angela!" shouted Tiffany. "It's not that difficult!"

Angela tried. She coaxed Dobbin, patted him and ordered him, but he stubbornly refused to budge. Even Linda tugging and pulling made no difference.

"Oh, Ang-er-la, you are funny!" tinkled Tiffany.

Then it happened. A horsefly landed on Dobbin's nose. Horseflies have a nasty bite and this one was no different.

Dobbin let out a shrill whinny and shot forward, dumping Linda in the dust.

"HEEELP!" screamed Angela, clinging on. Her riding hat had slipped over her eyes and she couldn't see a thing.

"WOAH, BOY!" she gasped. "Brake! Stop!"

But Dobbin didn't listen. He charged towards the first jump and took off. Angela felt like she was flying.

THUD! They hit the ground and Angela almost catapulted over Dobbin's head. Somehow she clung on, blindly. Dobbin cleared another jump and flew over the next three. Angela shook her hat back into place. She could hear voices, which almost sounded like cheering.

Dobbin wheeled round. He thundered at the last jump. It looked way too big. Angela shut her eyes…

"Arghhhhh…!"

KADUNK!

Angela gripped Dobbin's neck as they landed. The horse slowed to a stop, panting and snorting. Angela slid from the saddle and sat down heavily on the ground. Her legs were shaking and her hat was on sideways.

Suki and the others came rushing over. For some reason they seemed pleased that someone had beaten Tiffany.

"Well done, Angela!"

"That was amazing!"

"I didn't think you could ride!" they chattered.

Tiffany's face had turned as red as an overripe tomato.

"Goodness!" said Mrs Charmers. "That really was quite ... um ... astonishing."

"So Angela's the winner?" said Alice, looking at Tiffany. "She had the only clear round."

"Well, yes ... I suppose she did," said Mrs Charmers. Reluctantly she handed Angela the red rosette.

Everyone clapped, apart from Tiffany who looked like she might explode at any moment.

Angela beamed from ear to ear. She'd said all along that riding would come naturally to her. *Just wait until News Time on Monday,* she thought. This was one story she couldn't wait to share!

Neighbourhood
Watch!

Chapter 1

It was a rainy Saturday morning and Angela was waiting impatiently for her friends. She wandered into the kitchen.

"Mum, what's that new sticker in the front window?" she asked.

"That? It shows we belong to Neighbourhood Watch," replied Mrs Nicely. "We joined last week."

Angela frowned. "What's that?"

"It's a sort of club," explained Mrs Nicely. "The idea is we all keep an eye on our neighbours' houses."

"To see what they're up to?" asked Angela. It sounded fun. She'd like to know what people on her road were doing.

"No," said Mrs Nicely. "To watch out for anything suspicious – like someone nosing around or trying to get in."

Angela's eyes grew big. "You mean like a *burglar*!"

"I'm sure there aren't any burglars," said Mrs Nicely. "But if there were, Neighbourhood Watch will warn them to keep away."

Angela thought this over.

"Can I be in the club?" she asked.

"It's not for children," said Mrs Nicely.

"Why not?"

"Because it isn't!" groaned Mrs Nicely. The trouble with Angela was that her questions went on forever.

"I'd be good at watching," said Angela. "I can watch TV for hours."

"That's different," said Mrs Nicely. "But if you really want to help, we can all keep an eye out."

"What for?" said Angela.

"I don't know, anything out of the ordinary!" sighed Mrs Nicely. "Now please, go and find something to do!"

Angela went upstairs to wait for Maisie and Laura. It was still raining. From her bedroom window she could see the houses across the road. It would be easy to keep an eye on them.

Angela thought she'd be good at watching neighbours. Her mum was always saying it was rude to be nosey – but in the Neighbourhood Watch club, nosiness was encouraged! What was it her mum had said? Look out for anything "out of the ordinary". She could keep an eye on Bertie next door, but all he did was mess around with slimy slugs and worms.

Across the road at number 14, Mr Monk was sweeping his driveway.

Hmm, thought Angela, if anyone looked suspicious it was mean old Mr Monk. He had a tiny moustache, which looked like it was stuck on as a disguise. What's more, he hated children and didn't like them playing on the street. Maybe there was a reason? Maybe

Mr Monk had something to hide! *Someone ought to keep an eye on him,* thought Angela, and she had the perfect view from her window.

Chapter 2

Later Maisie and Laura arrived.

"What shall we do?" sighed Maisie, flopping on to the bed. "We can't go to the park in the rain."

"I know," said Angela. "We can do Neighbourhood Watching."

Maisie looked blank. "What's that?" she asked.

"It's like a club. You watch your neighbours to see if they're up to something," explained Angela.

"Isn't that spying?" asked Laura, doubtfully.

"No," said Angela. "Loads of grown-ups do it. You have to watch for anything suspicious – like robbing a bank or burglaring."

Maisie shrugged her shoulders. "There aren't any banks here," she said. "And anyway, who would we watch?"

"Mr Monk," said Angela, pointing to the house opposite.

"Not Mr Monk! He's *grouchy*!" moaned Laura.

Mr Monk had told them off many times – once for walking on his wall, and another time because he claimed their screaming and giggling was giving him a headache.

"Anyway, why HIM?" asked Maisie.

"Think about it," said Angela. "He never has any visitors. Why does he want everyone to keep away?"

"Because he's an old grump bag," said Maisie.

"Or because he's up to something," said Angela. "Anyway, do you want to be in the club or not?"

Laura and Maisie nodded. There was nothing better to do. Angela had borrowed her dad's binoculars so they could take turns keeping watch. As it was her idea, she went first.

It was amazing – with the binoculars she could see right into Mr Monk's house!

"What if he sees us looking?" whispered Laura.

"He won't," said Angela. "Not if we keep out of sight."

They kneeled down and peeped above the windowsill. Maisie was in charge of the notebook where they kept a record of everything Mr Monk did.

10.30 puts kettel on
10.35 Has koffee and biscit, (probably ginger nuts)
10.50 Gose upstares
10.53 Back in kitchin
11.00 ware's he gone now? To toilet?

Maisie put down her pencil and sighed heavily.

"This is *boring*," she grumbled. "He's not doing anything!"

"We can't give up or we'll miss something," said Angela.

"We've been watching for an hour," moaned Laura. "And all he's done is eat a biscuit."

Angela sighed. Neighbourhood Watching wasn't as exciting as she'd hoped. All the same, she was sure that Mr Monk couldn't be trusted. She stared through the binoculars. Mr Monk was in the kitchen, doing something at the sink. But he had changed his clothes. Now he was wearing a black jumper and trousers with a black balaclava over his head.

Angela's mum had said to look for anything out of the ordinary and this certainly was.

Suddenly Angela guessed the truth. "He's a BURGLAR!" she gasped.

"Who is?" asked Maisie.

"Mr Monk! Look!" said Angela. "He's dressed in black, just like a burglar!"

In films, spies and burglars were always dressed in black. It was so they couldn't be seen in the dark.

Maisie grabbed the binoculars. "Maybe he's wearing the hat to keep his ears warm," she suggested.

"Anyway, he wouldn't steal from his own house," Laura argued.

"Don't you get it?" asked Angela. "He went out and now he's back. I bet he's been breaking into someone's house!"

Maisie and Laura looked at each other. This was just like Angela – she was so dramatic!

"What about Mrs Monk?" said Maisie. "She'd know if he was up to something."

"But she's not there," said Angela. "We haven't seen her. I bet he waits till she's gone away and that's when he does it."

"Come on, Angela!" sighed Laura. "You don't have any proof!"

Angela raised her eyebrows. "Not yet," she said. "But I bet we can find some."

Chapter 3

For the next hour Angela watched the house like a hawk. Finally Mr Monk came out of the front door. He was still wearing the black top and trousers, but the balaclava was gone. Angela guessed that would have given him away. Burglars had to be careful.

"Quick!" she cried. "Now's our chance!"

"Angela!" cried Laura, but Angela was already rushing downstairs. By the time they caught up with her, she was outside Mr Monk's house.

"Oh, hi, Mr Monk!" she called out.

Mr Monk looked round. "Oh. What do you want?" he said, scowling.

Angela smiled. "How are you today?"

"I'm busy," snapped Mr Monk, unlocking his car.

"And how's *Mrs Monk*?"

"She's not here," sighed Mr Monk.

"Oh, not here!" repeated Angela. "But I expect you've got lots to do, haven't you? I bet you've been busy?"

Mr Monk looked at her as if she was raving mad. "What business is it of yours?" he growled. "Go and bother someone else!"

He got into his car, slammed the door and drove off.

"See?" Angela said to her friends. "He got really cross when I asked what he was doing."

Laura thought that Mr Monk seemed cross all the time. "Anyway, there's nothing we can do," she said.

"We can look for evidence," said Angela. "I bet he's got things hidden away – diamonds, jewels, stuff that he took."

"We shouldn't even be here!" moaned Laura. "Let's go before he comes back."

But Angela was wondering where Mr Monk would hide his loot. At the back of the house was a garage. She walked down the drive.

"Angela!" said Maisie. "You can't just go nosing round their house!"

"We're not *in* the house," said Angela. "And we're only looking. Come on!"

Laura and Maisie looked at each other in despair. They were mad to listen to Angela, it always ended in trouble – but they couldn't just walk off and leave her.

They found her poking around inside the garage. There were bikes, boxes, tools and a smell of oil and paint.

"Look at this!" gasped Angela. She reached into a box and pulled out a pair of silver candlesticks.

"STOLEN!" hissed Angela. "What did I tell you? These are worth millions!"

Laura stared. Maybe Angela was right? Now she really wanted to go back.

"There has to be more," said Angela. "Where's he hidden it all?"

"Let's go!" pleaded Laura.

But Angela wasn't listening. She'd caught sight of something through the garage window. Across the lawn was a freshly dug bed of earth. *Why would Mr Monk be digging*? thought Angela. Unless he had something he wanted to hide?

Chapter 4

Five minutes later, Angela was ankle deep in mud. She had found a spade in the garage and was looking for gold, silver or jewels buried under the earth. Laura kept watch by the garage. Maisie paced up and down restlessly.

"Angela, *come on,*" she begged. "You've made enough mess already!"

Angela wiped her dirty face and looked around her. There was quite a bit of mess. Soil was scattered across the lawn along with a number of plants that Angela had uprooted. There was no sign of any jewels. Still, Angela was sure that Mr Monk had buried something. Why else would he be digging in his garden?

Suddenly Laura let out a shriek. A car was coming this way.

"Quick!" she cried. "He's back! Run!"

"There's no time," said Angela, dropping the spade. "Hide in here!"

They made it in through the garage door just as Mr Monk's car pulled up on the drive. They found a smelly old blanket and crawled underneath, hardly daring to breathe. Mr Monk's heavy footsteps came up the drive.

CRUNCH,
CRUNCH,
CRUNCH!

Angela's heart was pounding. The footsteps stopped, then seemed to go past the door.

Angela and her friends crouched still, listening.

"Has he gone?" hissed Laura.

"I think so," whispered Angela.

"Let's get out while we can," said Maisie.

Keeping the blanket over their heads, they began to tiptoe forward. It was difficult to see where they were going.

"Where's the door?" whispered Laura.

"SHHH!" hissed Angela. "It's over—OUCH!"

They'd walked into something. Angela looked down. She could see a pair of large feet wearing brown leather sandals. Help! Only one person she knew wore sandals like that.

The blanket was whipped out of their hands. Mr Monk stood over them, his tiny moustache bristling.

"ARRGH!" screamed the girls.

"WHAT ARE YOU DOING IN HERE?" yelled Mr Monk. "I should call the police!"

"Don't!" whimpered Laura. "We didn't do anything."

Angela tried to sound brave. "If you call the police, we'll tell them what we know," she said.

"What?" snapped Mr Monk.

"We've seen you, creeping around in black, wearing a balaclava," said Angela. "You're a burglar!"

"A burglar? Is that what this is about?" said Mr Monk. "Not that it's any of your business, but these are my decorating clothes. I was painting the bedroom ceiling and I didn't want paint in my hair. That's why I was wearing a balaclava."

Angela felt her stomach sink. "But the silver candlesticks..."

"Mine," said Mr Monk. "And they're not real silver."

"And you dug up the garden to hide all your loot!" said Angela.

"Oh, yes, the garden," said Mr Monk.

He marched them across the lawn to the spot and pointed. "That's the flower bed I dug yesterday to plant with tulips," he said. "It was meant to be a special surprise for my wife. But *someone* has destroyed it!"

Angela opened her mouth, but for once nothing came out. The flowerbed was just a flowerbed and Mr Monk wasn't a burglar. Right now, though, he looked pretty mad.

"Right, here's the choice," he said. "We can go and tell your parents what you've been up to – or else..."

He held out the spade.

Angela gulped. "You wouldn't … bury us?"

"Don't tempt me," said Mr Monk. "No, I want this flowerbed tidied up and all the tulips replanted. And it had better be perfect. Mrs Monk's due home at four o'clock." He marched off back to the house.

Angela picked up the spade.

"ANGELA!" moaned Maisie. "What did we tell you?"

"You *never* listen," grumbled Laura.

Angela pulled a face. "It wasn't my fault. Anyone can make a mistake."

She looked at the flowerbed. They had better get on with it, she thought. Digging up a big pile of earth, she threw it over her shoulder.

"ARGHHH!"

"ANGELAAAAAAAAA!"

"Oops!" said Angela. "Sorry!"